Power Down, Little Robot

Anna Staniszewski

Illustrated by Tim Zeltner

HENRY HOLT AND COMPANY ✳ NEW YORK

Henry Holt and Company, LLC
Publishers since 1866
175 Fifth Avenue
New York, New York 10010
mackids.com

Library of Congress Cataloging-in-Publication Data
Staniszewski, Anna.
Power down, Little Robot / Anna Staniszewski ; illustrated by Tim Zeltner. — First edition.
pages   cm
Summary: "It's time to power down for the night, but Little Robot
isn't ready! He quickly opens his stalling program. Luckily, Mom Unit knows
exactly how to get him into his sleep module." —Provided by publisher
ISBN 978-1-62779-125-0 (hardback)
[1. Bedtime—Fiction. 2. Robots—Fiction.] I. Zeltner, Tim, illustrator. II. Title.
PZ7.S78685Po 2015   [E]—dc23   2014028419

Henry Holt books may be purchased for business or promotional use.
For information on bulk purchases, please contact the Macmillan Corporate and Premium Sales
Department at (800) 221-7945 x5442 or by e-mail at specialmarkets@macmillan.com.

First Edition—2015 / Design by Véronique Lefèvre Sweet
The artist used acrylic on plywood and a unique combination of stains and glazes
to create the illustrations for this book.
Printed in China by South China Printing Co. Ltd., Dongguan City, Guangdong Province

1 3 5 7 9 10 8 6 4 2

For mombots and dadbots everywhere
—A. S.

To J. J. and Jessie
—T. Z.

"Bedtime, my little robot!" Mom Unit calls.

I quickly open my stalling program.

"I am thirsty. Can I have a can of oil?" I ask.

"You have already gone over your daily limit," Mom Unit says. "It is time to power down for the night."

"All the other robots get to stay up late."
"You are the only robot I care about,"
she says. "Now hurry and clean your cogs."

I try to brush them at half my normal rate, but nothing gets past Mom Unit's sharp eye.

Before I know it, I am in my sleep module. It is time to move to Part II of my stalling program. "Will you read me a manual?"

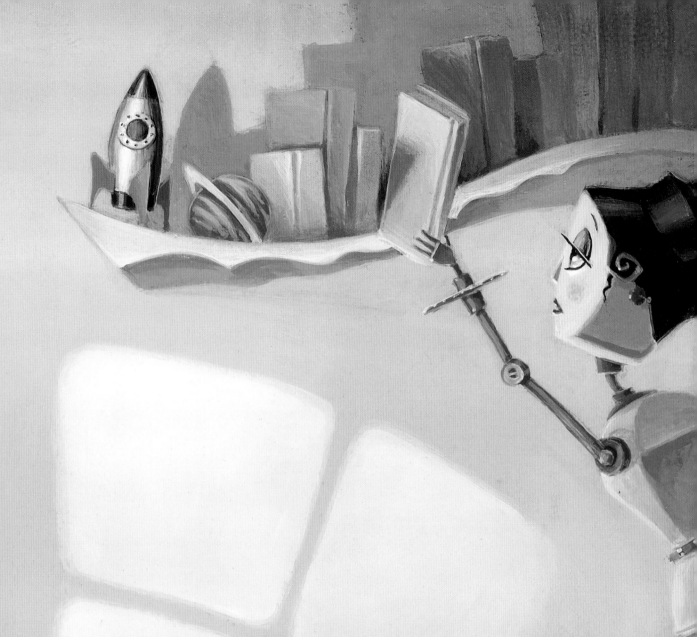

Mom Unit chooses the thinnest one
on the shelf.

"Can you tell me the story of how I
was manufactured?"

She fast-forwards through the
shortest version.

"How can I power down without my favorite toy?"

She digs him out from behind my pillow.

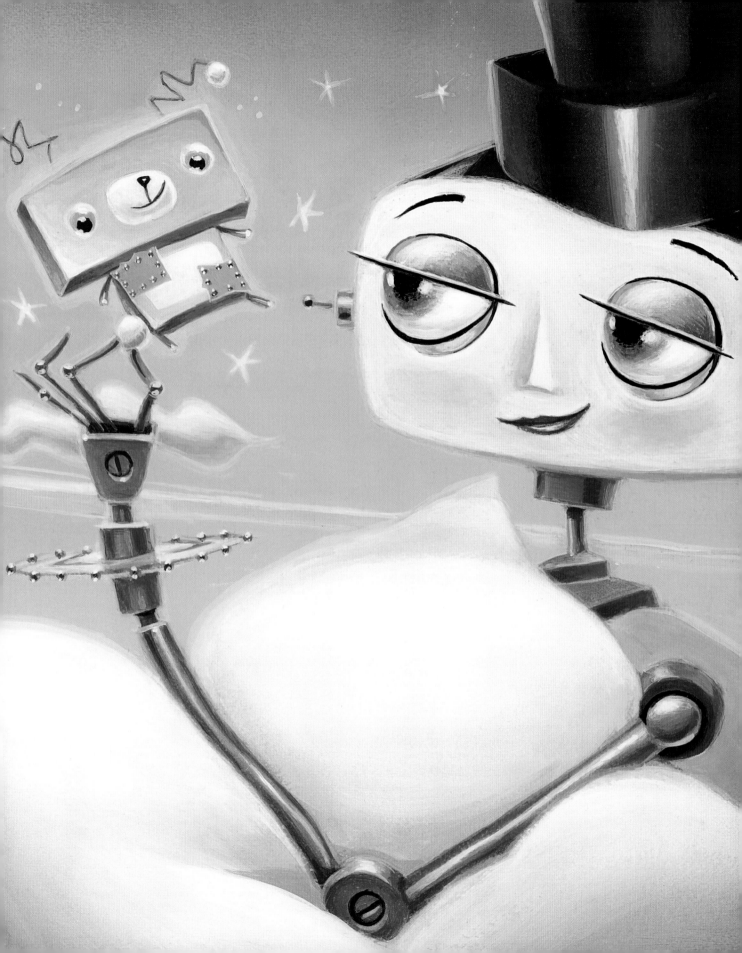

"All right now," she says.
"You must recharge."
"But I am not tired! Look.
My power level is still at yellow."

Mom Unit turns off
the light. The situation
is becoming serious.

"But I need to tell you a secret!"
I lower my voice to whisper volume.
"Did you know that a hummingbot flaps
its wings a million times a second?"

Mom Unit only laughs and clicks on
the night light.

"What if my dreams have error messages again?" I ask.

She promises to protect me.

"Did you check the closet for rust monsters?"

She scans the entire room. Twice.

"I think I forgot to brush
my cogs."
   She plays back the recording
from earlier.

"But—my circuits hurt!"
Mom Unit smiles. "Your
systems are functioning
normally."

She closes the door.

Once Mom Unit is gone, I wait exactly sixty-seven seconds.

Then I creep

down the stairs,

but I do not
get very far.

"Enough!" Mom Unit says. "If you do not power down now, you will lack energy for the botball game tomorrow. Do you want to interface with your friends or not?"

"Fine," I announce. "I will go to my module, but I will NOT power down."

Mom Unit tucks me in tight. The sleep module is soft and warm.

Maybe I could close my eyes for a millisecond. . . .

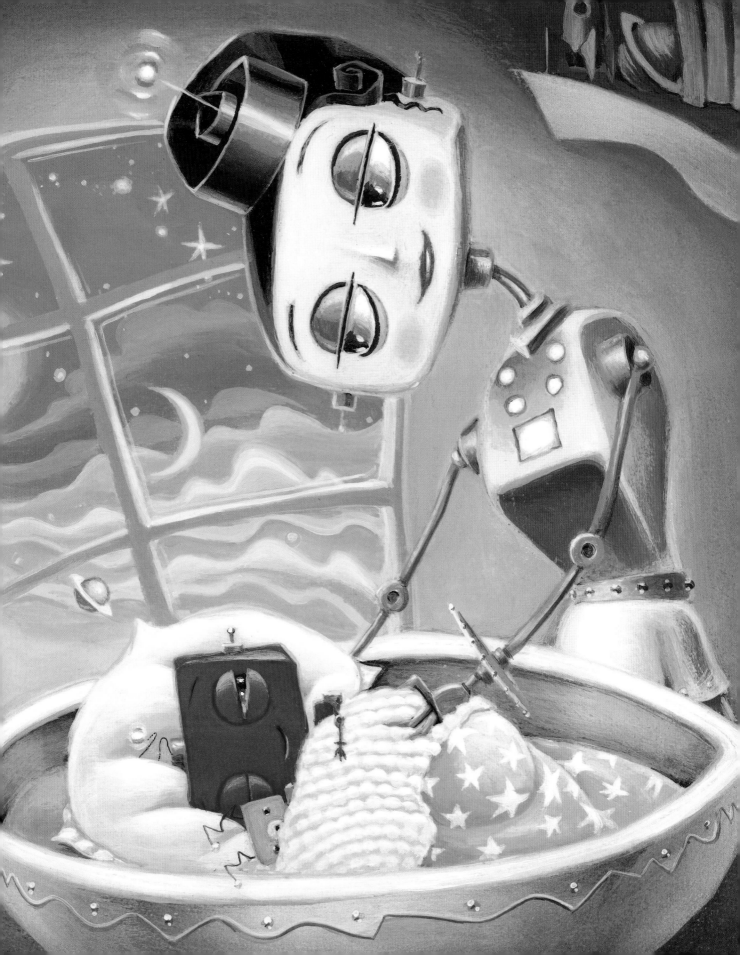

"Will you stay with me until I go into sleep mode?" I murmur.

Mom Unit smiles and clamps my hand in hers.

"Of course," she says. "Now power down, little robot."

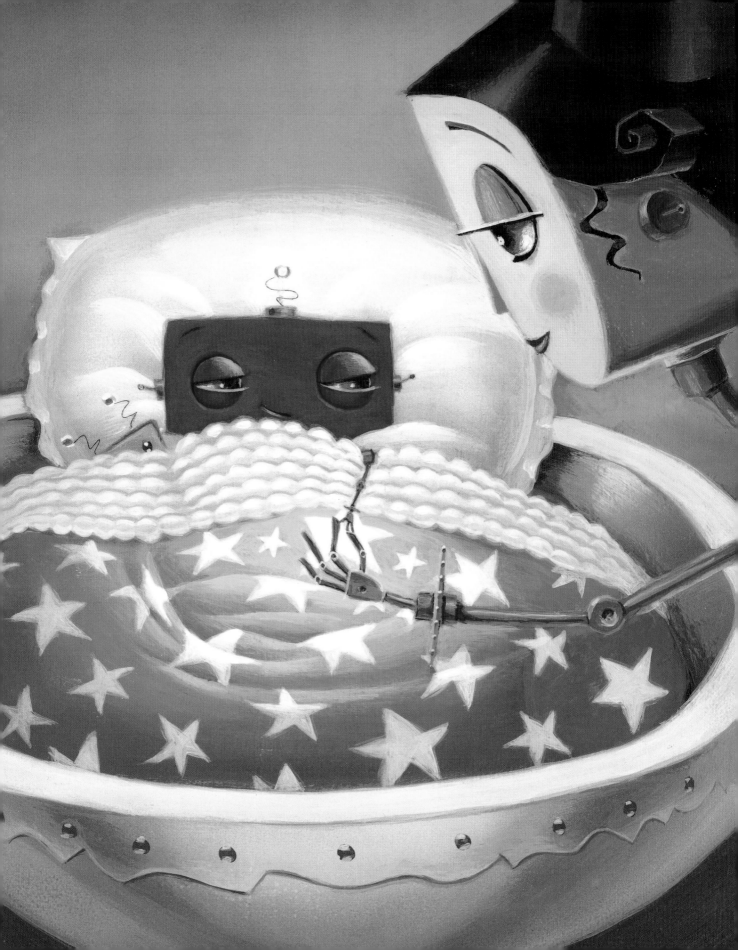

Dream sequence initiated.